ASK, ALICE

Illustrations by Richard Van Ingram
Story by Garry Somers

Blotter Books

Art copyright 2022 by Richard Van Ingram
Text copyright 2022 by Garrison Somers
First Printing 2022
This is completely and obviously a work of fiction.
Any similarity or resemblance to persons living, dead or undead is merely coincidental.

Ingram, Richard Van 1966 -
Somers, Garrison 1957 -
Ask, Alice
ISBN 979-8-9859878-0-5
Published in the United States by
Blotter Books
an imprint of The Blotter Magazine, Inc.
1010 Hale Street, Durham, NC 27705
Printed and bound in the USA

ASK, ALICE

ILLUSTRATIONS BY
RICHARD VAN INGRAM

STORY BY
GARRY SOMERS

"For Mark: Wish you were here.
And Bobbie: Glad you are."
- RVI

"Mom, this one is for you,
despite its being in no way your particular cup of tea"
- GS

Ask, Alice

What star this is I've not a clue,
I trust the work astronomers do.
The ship's computer has decided
that we might drop in uninvited.
My fellow 'nauts are still asleep,
for air is precious - space is deep.
Were they awakened they'd not be thrilled
to find one of the crew - me - killed.
And you who gaze at twinkling lights
there's something out here...I think it bites.
I love adventure, I find it fun,
but now I wish I'd brought a gun.
Listen; 'neath the rattles and hums,
I hear a growling. Here it comes!

from "Zero Grav in the Void One Evening" by E. R.

At 217-254-20-32 the alarm went off and the extruded shatter-resistant polystyrene hatch slid back with a whir of servos and a click that no one heard. She opened her eyes and because it was in her line of sight became aware of the place where the noise erupted but could provide no meaning to it nor connect how the flashing orange luminescent characters corresponded to the auditory blasts of the alarm or what they represented. Or who she was or what was her name. All was normal. Human Cryogenic Transport Process did not suspend in a dream state. Anyone in dream state for such extended periods of time would become clinically insane. How the ubiquitous *they* knew this was unfortunately empirical.

Oh, I'm Alice sat up exactly thirty minutes later, groggy with such a post-slowed heart and lowered core temperature sleep induced headache that she popped two gel-coated and un-foiled ibuprofen tablets conveniently sitting on the table next to her cryorack to combat it. They tasted, in a word, old.

She could suddenly talk and so croaked "alarm off," and it was.

She then coughed up some old-ibuprofen flavored spit and spoke the next word that popped into her head. "Backup?" The ship's artificial intelligence, named...*Del!* didn't speak, but printed out her itinerary at her cryorack as it always did, because she had pre-programmed that she preferred to read rather than listen to his soft male monotone report. And now she could read. Two Hundred Seventeen? My goodness! That made her a whopping...here came fully-formed arithmetic, thank you...Two Hundred Thirty-Nine solar years old. No record, of course, but a worthy accomplishment nevertheless. What in the living *hell*, was her next thought. We're not yet halfway home. Holy crap.

She shucked off her underpants and padded unsteadily to the shower. No real reason; she wasn't dirty, even from such a long suspended animation – her hair had stopped growing when she slept, as had her nails, and those little mites that squatted in people's eyelids and feasted on sloughed skin and even chewed on the dried salt of tears had been eradicated when she went through decontamination prior to flight. Still, a shower was what she always had when she woke up – hurrah, more memory!

Bending over, she plucked off the sticky sensors on her calves, thighs, buttocks and biceps. They were no fun to shower with because they contained tiny batteries that sent electrical charges while she was in cryo so that those larger muscles didn't atrophy, and being batteries they tended to short out in water. She tossed them on a bench and climbed under the shower-heads. The water was wet, and there was plenty of it, or, rather, there was a lot of water streaming down, plashing against her scalp, rolling down her skin, drizzling down into the suction drain at her feet, tracking back to H_2O
containment where electrolysis precipitated out particulates, filtered the wetness molecules

through an osmotic still, and collected and re-
turned the same, renewed water to the shower
pump for warming up and re-draining pleasantly
onto her head and face and breasts and rump.
Her knees wobbled, an unfamiliar combination
of pleasant feeling and weakness.

Air jets puffed against her wet skin as soon as
she turned off the H_2O.

Ooh, chilly.

She tapped the thermostat up two notches,
and was rewarded with warm air. In ninety seconds she was both clean and dry. She would have
fetched a new pair of panties and some 'ralls, but
she couldn't remember where the clean clothes
were. Sporadic memory loss on the short term
was a side-effect of slo-lo sleep. It would all come
back to her, she knew. Or at least she thought
she knew. Alice smiled to herself at the paradox.

Happily, the ibuprofens had not completely
deteriorated with age. Her headache was now
replaced by hunger. She requested Del to make

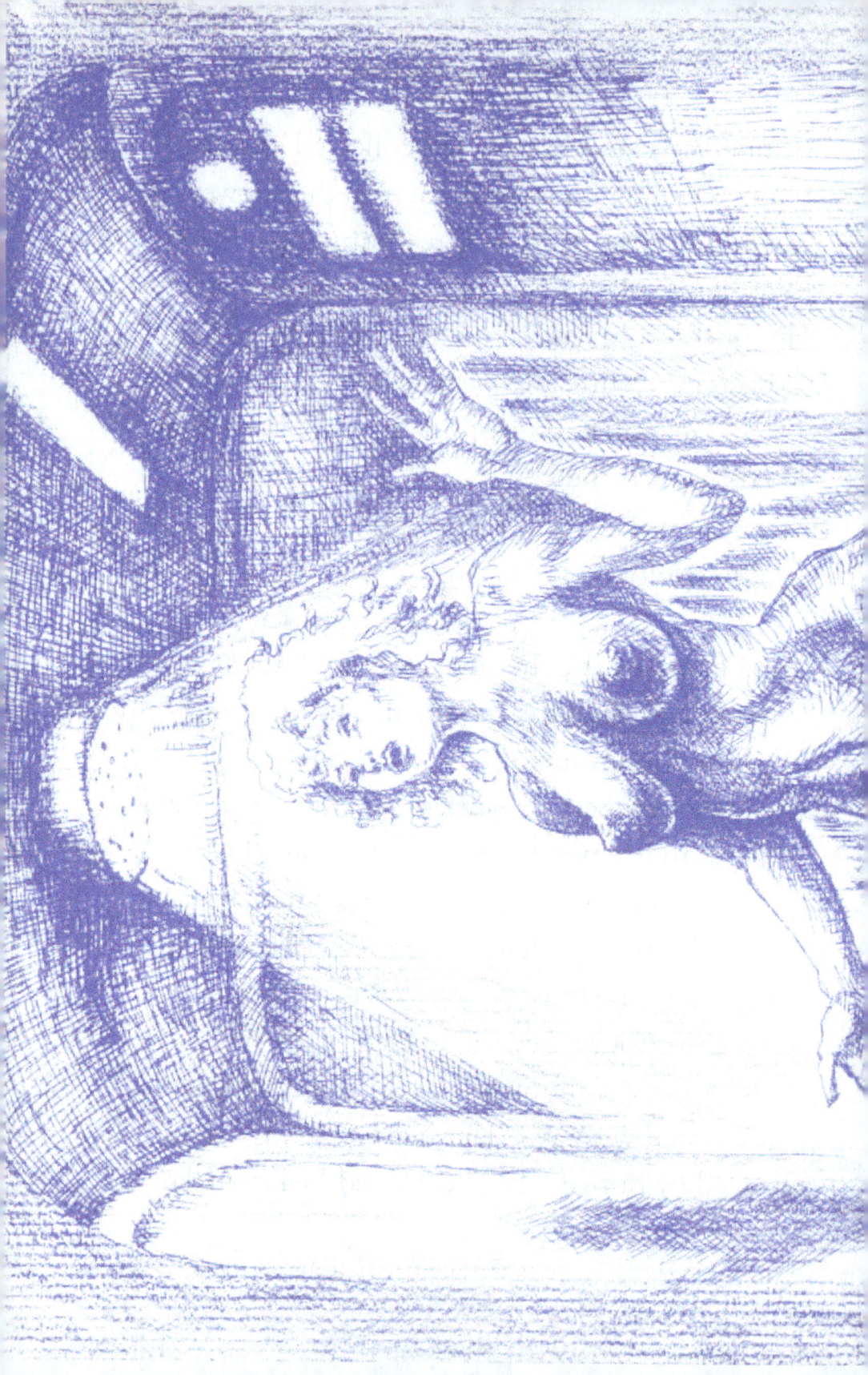

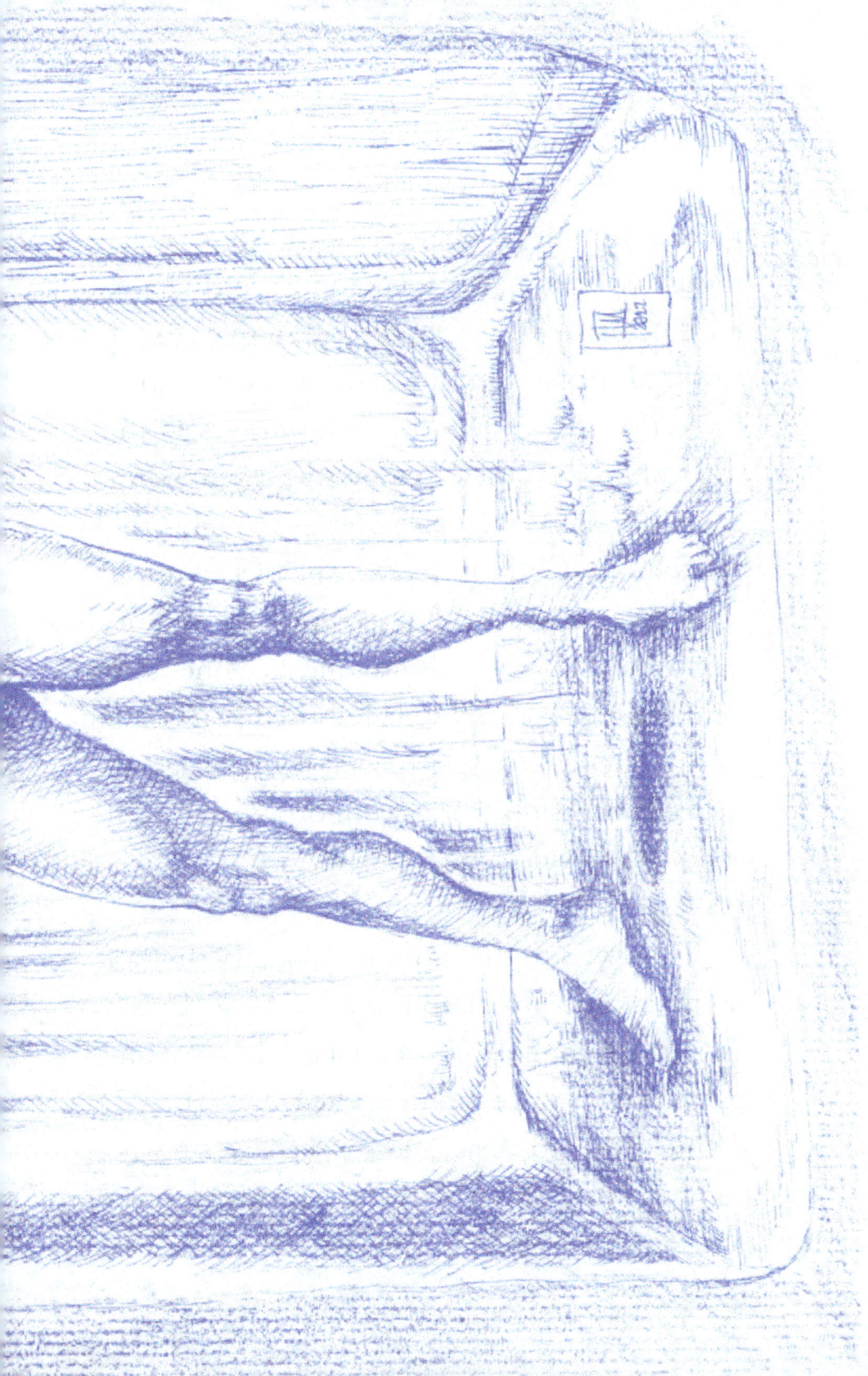

her some breakfast. He said nothing, but within a minute she could smell eggs and bacon. Preprogramming. That is a nice feature, she thought. Nothing better than the perfume of a meal before eating. Oh, they wouldn't be real eggs and bacon. But if she was remembering correctly, a tricky question, both the ersatz and the real McCoy, they'd be pretty nice mock-up comestibles. A quiet *ping* over by the table told her that her food was ready. She picked up the itinerary print-out and sat down to eat and read. She chewed slowly and carefully, like one might who had just had a couple hundred years of dental anesthesia. The plastic seat felt cool against her bare backside, not uncomfortable at all. It's good to be awake, she thought.

There was nothing on the itinerary that was useful. Normal backup was a brief high-level almanac of home events and a catalog of company news. At the moment she could barely define the word *home*, and suspected that company news, even if she had a vague perception of it, was mostly corporate jibberish. Subspace communications was time consuming and expensive, requiring dedicated satellite directional lasers and so beyond place-time expectations for the vessel she found little that interested her. Apparently she'd been awakened because of an anomalous signal, with instructions to investigate. Natural cynicism kicked in. For crying out loud, she thought, if this turned out to be a fluttering pulsar or some such cosmic foolishness, she was going to throw a spanner at something. Of course, if that was all this was why couldn't Del investigate? Tell me that in the century and a half since mission start, we hadn't gotten any closer to trusting our machinery. All that backlash from the first AI's, God help us. Well, apparently people at home were still idiots. She flipped over the print-out flimsy. Reading through the paper, the block print letters were upside down, and backwards. Far more intriguing this way.

Alice finished her meal without engaging in further thinking. Just letting her memory slowly return and hand-eye coordination required to mop up eggs with faux-toast was entertainment enough.

She finally found her clothes – a clean gray cotton shift and a pair of short pants - and

strolled to the ship's bridge. It was hardly worthy of being called that – just an armored panic-room with some stools sitting at a pair of terminals and an auto-pilot override joystick. She stared at the antiquated thing, with its thumb-switch and trigger. Silly really. No human could ever successfully do a manual steer of this vessel. For crap sake, it was the size of, what did they used to call those old urban dwellings? Skyscrapers? You had to do the trigonometry for 3D linear countermotion while maintaining gimbals and trim and

know all the physics for acceleration and mostly it was like trying to herd kindergartners. Frankly, I'd rather crash, she thought. She called Del to the left-hand terminal and requested a vicinity scan, out to one parsec. The closest planet was the exact opposite of earthnorm (sudden recollection – a classmate she'd had who they called

EarthNorm, because he'd failed his qualifying exams multiple occasions until finally he'd aged-out of the program and gone on to...what? Land-scape repair! An industry set to putting right all the planet's scars from two-hundred-plus years of the so-called industrial revolution. The very definition of irony.) Back to this planet, though. Oh, boy. Silicate dust storms drifting over sulfur plains. Ammonia bubbling to the surface jetted away in the hot chemical wind to form wispy blue-green clouds. It might have been pretty, if you could live through it and your eyes didn't melt out of your skull. Nothing down there worth the time/distance from a mineral perspective. So what's the deal? Something new? She tapped the key-sheet with her fingertip.

"Think, girly," Alice said under her breath. She asked Del to show the master contract page for emergency wake-up priority specifications. Scanning it, there was nothing she hadn't already known and signed off. Was it a mistake? "Show me the wake command," she asked. Del complied. There was no explanation. Shit. The code-string for the wake command? Del streamed the pages of characters and spaces. Re-stream and stop on comments. There it was. An Extra-terrestrial Life Form look-see. A freaking *ELF*-hunt.

"Well, go ahead, then," she told Del. "Let's see what's up."

It might have been convenient to throw down a probe at the grim and desolate planet, but she didn't want to hear the grief about cost impact. Not even a distant (temporally as well as spatially) three quarters of a century from now. For all she knew, they would take it out of her bonus, somewhere down that road, so to speak. And there was no way Alice was going to thaw out any of the others to schedule a group piss-and-moan festival. She would solve this herself. The truth be told, they were assholes, her crew. One and all. She groaned inwardly at the thought of waking up Cappie, or that ding-a-ling girl handling medical, what's her name? Cappie, the ship's actual science officer, had the personality of a cup of warm orange-ade, with a matching intellect, and if the

company had meant for him to be summoned for one of these exercises, they would have programmed Del to wake him instead of her, right?

"So, what's left that a girl can do?" she murmured to herself with a shrug, pushing a loose bit of short, blonde hair off her forehead. She keyed in the command and Del complied. She thought she felt the slight judder of the remote bucket jettisoning from the freighter's mining bay, knowing that the mass of the great ship was far too large for this to be so. Residual species memory was what that was. We're just fleas on this old dog.

She leaned back in the chair, closed her eyes and rubbed her temples with her fingertips to stimulate blood flow. Or not. The bucket would do what remotes do best – drop through the atmosphere spinning and swirling around the planet – a beautiful, toxic, caustic mist – and extract a sample of whatever it was told to. In this case, *whatever it was told to* was that damn close to hard-coded requirement to investigate the life indication.

Freaking *loud* alarm this time.

Alice jumped. Had this been a normal workday – reveille, three squares, work shift and an evening debrief – she might have peed herself. As it was she was still dehydrated from cryo, and the AI's buzzer merely startled her out of her reverie, staring at chemical compounds and assembly language.

"Yes, Del?" she asked as calmly as she was able. "Do you need something?"

The screen in front of her went blank and then diplayed a motion warning. Something in the house, eh?

Inanimate? A falling cardboard carton of nails or badly stacked paint-cans?

No.

The bucket was still three hours away from completing the round-trip to the surface of this planet on a good day with a tailwind. When it retrieved the cargo it would perform a light-lift around the planet to pick up velocity for breaking gravity in order to save fuel.

What the hell was this, then? Isolate, if you please.

Supply room, recyclables. Crew-space. Inside the firewall, as it were. So it was time for some exercise.

Alice slipped on a pair of nonskid soles and picked up the little handheld everyone called *the brick.* Hung the device around her neck by its plastic lavaliere. "Throw it all over on here, Del," she said, and he uploaded the data to the brick.

When you got right down to it, you had to admit this freighter was a distinctly creepy place. Some of the twisting passageways were large and airy; others were apparently manufactured for use by illogical Lilliputians. She hated tight squeezes – her predisposition to claustrophobia had been re-treated with chemo-hypno-therapy prior to this tour – and the company's decision whether to adequately light a space or not was haphazardly applied at best. If she hadn't known better, she would have labeled it a government ship, but it was a second-class cargo cruiser, or at least it had been when it was built. And although that was a good two hundred years earlier, Alice doubted that things were much better now. A ship was like a city. Even those with the best laid plans had unexpected twists and turns.

The supply room was a silly name, really, for it was an open area so large that it created its own weather. Pulley chains dangled from high above, dripping with moisture. They rattled in har-monic sympathy with the freighter's impulse engine, giving the place its own private scary-music.

Alice rubbed back down her annoyingly hard nipples and shivered – the space was cooler than the bridge because there were no workstations here. She wiggled her fingers to relieve their tension and lifted the brick. "Update on motion," she whispered.

One, your location, Del replied, letting her know that he saw her.

"What motion since previous update?"

None.

"Was original reading an anomaly?"

Unknown.

Feels like a goose chase, she thought. Hate this shit.

"Show me the spot, Del." Del displayed the grid where the motion had been detected. Alice opened the side of the brick and removed a charged defense pen. No bigger than a stylus, it packed a disabling jolt of electricity, delivered either through contact or proximity and supposedly enough to disable either human-sized live or AI problems.

"Lights?" she asked Del. He flicked on a couple of bulbs in the distance.

"That's it?" she asked. Del said nothing. Shaking her head, Alice stepped forward, with the defense pen in one hand and the brick in the other, set for motion recognition and heat registration. OK, then. More than just a little bit spooked. In spite of the cool, a dribble of sweat rolled down the small of her back. Damn it. What was going on here?

She felt it more than saw it. A flash of dark scooting across the darker dark of the deck. The motion sensor jumped from silent to continuous ping. Fast! The electric pen wasn't going to help even a little bit.

"What the hell is it, Del?" No answer. Useless computer.

Back the hell out, Alice, she scolded herself. Right now. In the gloom, the mysterious thing was now skulking stealthily towards her.

"Oh, for crap sake!" At the very moment Del decided to enlighten her about Chessie, Alice leaned over and picked up the fat, furry ball. It purred and rubbed its face against hers. She growled, partly at the cat for scaring the shit out of her, and partly at Del. A little faster on the uptake next time, if you don't mind, she thought. She tucked the electric stun-pen in her pocket.

The ship's cat was an orange tom, and a clone. No reason for him to be aboard, except that someone way back had said it was OK, or more likely that it was not *not*. Chessie, however, experienced none of the iffy joys of cryo-sleep. Instead, in each generation, a DNA sample was taken and put in cryo medical storage. When Chessie shook this mortal coil, as all cats do, a new Chessie was cooked in the primordial soup of a makeshift clone lab the crew had set up in a corner of the health clinic. Cappie, the smarty-pants, had even automated it, so that the recycling command for an expired and decomposing Chessie set the cloning-soup process in motion. Disgusting, when it came right down to it. So Alice didn't think about it, other than to wonder how old this one was. She liked the cat...cats... *this* cat a lot. Somehow, she didn't know or care why, the cat survived generations alone aboard the ship without the companionship of humans, unsuspended in animation and yet still domesticated bordering on friendly. Something in cat-nature, she surmised. Or perhaps her own. Alice often found him more satisfying to talk to than most of the others in the crew. Particularly interesting because he was also *upgraded*. One of the Barneys, the freighter-ship's engineers, possibly as a joke, had inserted an RI (recognition-interpretation) nano-chip into the original Chessie before the outbound cryo, converting the cat's occasional vocalizations into English, and the cloning process included chip-insertion, and re-insertion during subsequent clonings. In other words, Chessie no longer meowed. Although the chip's function had deteriorated somewhat, when the cat *spoke* it was with a languid, yowling sort of creole-English, as if he were from the deepest, most Southern part of the old United States back on Earth. Alice felt it made the cat decidedly more interesting.

More interesting than any of the other members of the crew, that is. Ah, Cappie wasn't such a complete rat-bastard as she made him out to be. She hadn't been fair earlier. Actually he had the personality of a whole pitcher of warm orange-ade. But he was too full of himself by half (a tricky unit of measure!) for his own good, had a problem understanding the concept of privacy, and left his shaved whiskers sitting in the bathroom sink, like tea-leaves waiting to be discerned.

That last might have been the company's fault for not having installed more modern facilities, right? And in a pinch, he was passable in the rack, she supposed, considering the choices. Stumpfl, the ship's captain, was a stiff without a stiffy. Wilson was an actual empty suit. God, you just gotta hate a company rep, right? And the two Barneys: engineering savants that picked their noses. Not the worst habit in the world. But hiding the boogies under the pillow? Congratulations, now *that* was the worst habit. Edelman preferred video lovers, alternating gender selection on a whim. And that medical girl, the ding-a-ling, with a voice like fingernails scraping. What was her damned name, anyway?

"Next time, old Chessie," she said to the cat as it washed its face with a white-gloved paw. "Next time I'll look at the guest list before I say yes to attending a mad tea party. For revenge, I should wake them all up for this shindig, and go back to sleep myself." The cat, despite its ability to respond, turned and began washing the other side of its face. It turned out some aspects of feline civility could not be overcome by science.

Alice made a random mental note to do something unbecoming to ding-a-ling girl before she went back into cryo, after all of this was laid to rest.

The brick pinged. *Please return for incoming.* Incoming? How could there be incoming subspace communications? Nobody yet knew that she was awake. Curiouser and curiouser. Holding Chessie close and gently chucking him under the chin, she made her way back to the bridge.

She placed a bowl of soy liquid on the floor for the cat, who wisely sniffed at it before giving it a tentative lick. "Good" but no "Thank You." Oh, well. Alice poured a glass for herself. The slightly salty stuff was nothing at all like milk, even if you held your nose and closed your eyes. She guessed you had to be a cat to pretend to enjoy it.

"What the living hell is going on here?" Man's voice, an odd combination of both deep and airy. Alice turned too quickly and her head

swam like her thoughts were sloshed with cold water.

Shit.

"Who authorized you...?" the man growled.

It was Cappie, standing behind her, hands on hips, frowning.

"No one, sir," Alice said. "I was the only one awake. Awakened, I mean."

"Really? That seems...unlikely," said Cappie, and somewhat flamboyantly waved the flat of one hand along his showered, shaved and beige 'ralled self.

"I didn't know."

Cappie shook his head, and she could suddenly smell his aftershave, as if it were a thick fog slowly wafting out from him.

"Status report," he said, looking up at the ceiling, as if that was where Del was. No response from the computer.

"I think," she started to explain the problems she'd been having with Del, but Cappie cut her off with an impatient wave of that same hand.

"Who released the bucket?"

"I did. Sir."

"I'm disappointed," Cappie said and slowly shook his head.

Of course he is, Alice thought. And now you're going to have to pay for a bucket if it doesn't come back in mint condition. She started to do the painful math in her head.

They faced each other and she wondered what to say next. Considered crossing her arms so her hard nipples would cut it out, but didn't move. Cappie just stood there.

"I'm disappointed," he said again.

A slight breeze blew the wisp of Alice's hair ticklingly across her brow once more. She cursed herself as she felt that she coquettishly pushed it back out of her face.

A woman's voice from the hallway. Like... fingernails on a, what?

"It's a residual anomaly, Alice dear."

The ding-a-ling medico. Oh, please, no, Alice thought. Not now.

"I'm sorry?" she said.

"He's not there."

"Who's not there."

"Cappie. Not really there."

"Status report," said Cappie, still most defiantly *there*. He waved the flat of his hand along his 'ralls. Again. She huffed the musky stink of his aftershave. Again.

Shit.

Alice remembered, vaguely, that there had been a class she'd attended which included information about potential short, *middling*, and long-term after-effects of extended cryo. As different "sleep" chemicals were developed, supposedly to make things safer or any number of adjectives less unpleasant, these had been introduced to the human cryogenic transport process through a poke-and-hope methodology. *Residual anomaly* must have been one of those effects. She couldn't remember.

"He's just a multi-sensory hallucination," said ding-a-ling. Flick! Cappie was gone.

"OK," said Alice. "Wonderful." That's all I need, a Cappie-gram haunting me.

"Not just Cappie."

Ask, Alice

Alice blinked. She hadn't said that aloud, had she?

"Yes, Alice dear. Me, too," said the medico. "My fingernail-scraping voice. On something. But of course, you've already figured that out."

No, she hadn't, but she smiled at the punchline. She closed her eyes and shook her head. When she opened them again, the ding-a-ling's head was resting on a pedestal, rolling from side to side like a horrorshow Marie Antoinette, smiling widely at her.

"See?"

Yes, she saw. Go away, she thought, and the medico winked out of existence.

"Shut off the brick," she told Del. The device shimmered and faded. In front of her the display monitor flickered to life. Now what's happening?

A text message. Less likely to be corrupted by stellar flares and corresponding neutrino bursts. She sat down to read. Attn: SciOff...

SubCom transmissions from Earth to this point went on something like a two-and-a-half year journey. Indeed, no real argument in the classical sense of the concept was possible between mining labor and mining management, and therefore the contract was almost always brought into play. *Subject to the Requirements of the Company* was the clause that was the real stinker. It could mean almost anything, and it was rumored it had been exercised in defense of

both doing something, and punishment for having done that very same thing. Alice now thanked god that the others weren't actually awake. They would have fussed from one end of the freighter to the other about how to respond. *That wasn't what the contract said. That's not fair.*

You must be on their side. Let's vote. Eventually
everyone would grow tired, and a consensus
would be reached. Then after a bit of rest,
disappointment with the results would set in
and tempers would flare again, but by then the
communication response was on its way back to
Earth. *Were bonuses affected? How could they ever*

understand the difficulties out here? Frustration
inevitably reigned supreme...out here.

    Ah, so, asshole. So it seemed the company
must have known that the freighter would stop
here. This had been part of the mission plan
from the beginning. Based, perhaps, on a signal

picked up by some other company vehicle, some-how remaining a tightly guarded secret; double-plus crypto-coded into the computer. Just waiting for this ship to pass by on its return path, to send a command to *pull over, pal.* How do you like that for audacity? And freaking glacial patience, now that you mention it.

What was that first line? SciOff. The message was for Cappie. But hallucinations to the contrary, he wasn't even awake.

"When was the last time someone made a mistake like that, Chessie old boy?" she asked the cat, which now ignored the dish and was instead weaving around her feet. *I don't care,* the cat drawled, eyes half-closed, looking up at her, which Alice concluded meant "All the time. Mistakes are your kind's best thing."

OK, maybe human error, then. But think, she said to herself. How long must it have taken for the freighter to slow down? Even with an atomic engine, how much precious fuel did it use to bring this much mass to a stop in this system, synchronously following a planet around its sun? Plenty of time to make a simple decision about who to wake. So. Maybe it was an AI glitch. That was a tad more disturbing, actually. AI error was statistically rare, and chiefly the result of environmental issues – damp, caustic atmosphere, metallic micro-dust, hyper-magnetic environment. More often than not the mistake turned out to be a diagnostic conflict, or not an error at all but rather a...misunderstanding between programmed request and response. Had they meant for Cappie to be unthawed instead of her, but Del made such a *mistake?* Or had Del made a crew skill logic decision that she should be awakened instead of Cappie, based on heuristic analysis? She sat there, tapping a fingernail on the keysheet. She hesitated to ask. Then did it anyway.

"So why was I awakened?" she asked Del.

Because there was a signal, read the screen.

"Why was I awakened?" she repeated with the italics emphasis on "I."

Because there was a signal.

"Did you know that there would be a signal?"

I received the signal, read the screen, with just the merest hint of textual brat.

"Del," she sighed. "Did you know before you heard it that there might be a signal?" No answer.

"Del, why did you not awaken Cappie?"

Because you were already awake.

"Shouldn't Cappie have been awakened?"

Perhaps, but you were already awake.

Holy crap, Alice thought. Perhaps? What is up with the attitude? It's like arguing with my mom. Anyhow, somehow, Del had chosen to wake her instead of Cappie, even though his instructions were to wake the science officer. This was so fucked up.

"Del, is there something in the bucket?"

Yes.

"What?"

Something.

Goods? Goods was standard terminology for anything that the company would consider worthwhile mining. Ore of pure enough quality to warrant an expensive excursion into space. But Del did not respond.

Ask, Alice

"What the hell is it, Del?" The computer still didn't respond. *For crying out...*

Funny how exhausting suddenly not having something useful was when you were used to that useful thing. Like a trick knee, or a good memory, when they acted up, you sometimes felt like all of the rest of you was broken. Pulling the keysheet close, she tapped out the command for computer self-diagnostics, hardware and software.

An interminable twelve seconds. The report ran, then failed to complete. Alice felt the turn of the crank on her last nerve. She tapped the keysheet again. No response. The diagnostics commands didn't report at all. Alice frowned deeply. Someone – something – had fouled this up pretty good. Diagnostics never failed – not while *power ran to the box* as the old saying went. And the AI couldn't touch the diags, because they were...distinctly firewalled from the functional programming of the AI. In other words, Del couldn't actually see the diagnostics code, or them checking him for problems. But somehow Del still worked and the diagnostics didn't. The

AI done gone rogue, pard.

"What's in the bucket, Del?" she asked again, surprised by the shrillness of her own voice and the ludicrousness of repeating the query.

Something.

"Something bad?"

Yes.

"Well, then, maybe you shouldn't let the bucket come aboard."

No answer.

"Del, don't let it come aboard."

I cannot comply. As those words displayed, the bucket re-entered the deployment slot. A slight judder as the freighter's gyros re-adjusted to the weight. Too late. You pays your money and you takes your chances...

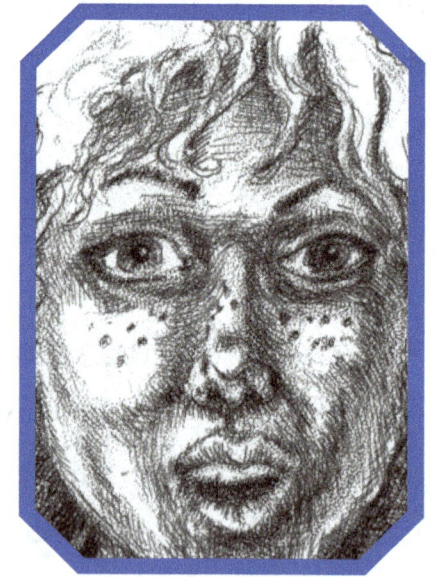

"Can you identify?"

No answer.

"Del," she tried one more time. "Are we in danger?"

No

Not quite precise enough.

"Am I in danger?"

Yes.

Shit.

Alice had had the willies before. Back when she was in tertiary school there had been a boy who didn't choose to understand the meaning of the word no, or even the command *back off, asshole!* The boy had decided he was in love, and came to her room and held a needle-gun – the kind of thing used for giving vaccinations – alternately to his own head and hers while he revealed his longing and loss and other emotions to her and the security and some headshrinkers and the vid crew of a local news bureau. The thing was loaded with some home-assembled poison. That had been fairly touch-and-go. Finally, loverboy had gotten tired and the vax-pistol was heavy so he'd let it swing down to his side for a moment and she'd chopped him in the throat with her fist, cracking his pharynx and making his throat so swiftly swell that he couldn't breathe. He'd probably actually wanted to shoot her at that point, but she had kicked the hypodermic handgun away when he dropped it from the onset of surprising pain. This was a little bit like that, she decided. Her legs wanted to run, but where? The freighter was an island. Sure, she could run, burn off all of this adrenochemical energy, but she'd be no further from the problem. So her toes wriggled in her slip-ons and she felt a little bit sick to her stomach. Keep thinking, though, she told herself. Odd consideration about that boy, who the emergency medical services had had to rescue in the end from her, and not the other way 'round. He was long dead, wasn't he? His bones in the ground for a century now, somewhere far away from here, turned to dust.

Her calm tested to new limits, Alice inquired again as to the nature of the threat, but either Del didn't know or wasn't saying. It was ridiculous to have this kind of security/insecurity, but that was that.

"Can you show me what is in the bucket?" No answer.

"Show me." No answer. Not directly disobeying, but petulant and insubordinate.

New issue: was Del really still subordinate to her? More to the point, had he ever been? Maybe in some warped company view, and with the right set of circumstances, he was the authority here. How messed up was that? Alice could feel the dampness in her armpits now, as she raised her arm and knuckled back hair that wasn't at all in her face.

Then she suddenly smelled something sweet, a marvelously strange perfume. Her cryo-addled memory couldn't place it, though. She groaned aloud. "What is that?" *Coffee*, read the screen. In his new status as adapted-in-thinking machine, Del had chosen to brew some ersatz coffee. Alice followed her nose to the crew table. *Ding*. And there it was. There was one thing about the food

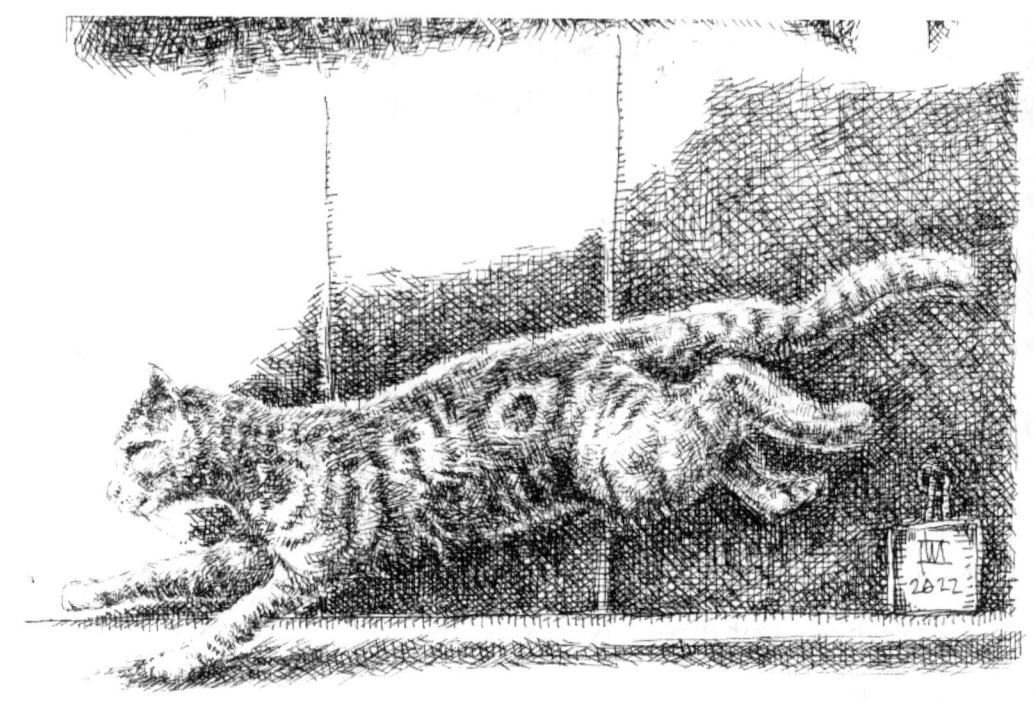

simulators. Someone must have decided that a
good cup of hot coffee was an absolutely *inalien-
able* right.

You never know what circumstances are going
to evolve to get you home, she thought with a
crooked smile, and sipped at the coffee. OK,
then. I have to go see what the bloody bucket
brought back. Ha. Say that five times fast....

Biohazard! Del said with a brief whoop of a

siren. *Containment protocol breach.* Immediately spooked by the sudden noise Chessie galloped down a passageway with a yowl that sounded a lot like *Oh, shit, oh shit, oh-shit.*

"Seal level Z security doors," Alice commanded. She shook her head slowly. Level Z would further compartmentalize the ship with airtight armor. This was chiefly used in the unlikely event of a fire or hull-skin breach. The ship was nuclear, of course, and because air could be controlled and localized vacuums created, there were few other combustibles of a total-annihilation-by-fire nature, but it was old-school security function.

Biohazard is in ventilation. Well, every scenario had an Achilles heel. Ventilation was compartmental but not armored.

"Did whatever-it-was tear into the ventilation?"

Yes.

"Identify?" she asked.

Danger, Del said, with another brief, sharp alarm-whoop.

Damn me, somebody's in the house, Alice

thought. Her head hurt, a stress headache crawling up the back of her neck. She realized that she had been ducking down as she looked at the monitor, as if gunfire was blazing over her head and tucking in would somehow protect her. She relaxed her neck and felt the pain slowly release.

Think! There were no guns on board the freighter. Nothing with high-velocity projectile launch capability. Mining drills were not hand-tools. She needed something to disable or destroy the thing that the bucket had brought back. More than the security pen. Something potentially deadly.

"Suggestions?" she asked Del. The computer was silent for a moment.

Abandon ship.

Not an option. Abandon ship and no one came for you. That was common knowledge. It was too damned expensive, and took too long. The company was more likely by far to come with a remote-operation tug and fetch the mined ore left derelict by her when she abandoned ship. So forget that. Not to mention, the others were still in suspended animation. To get them awake and into the life-boat pod swiftly was out of the question. And why should she abandon ship, anyway?

"What did you let on board?

Del couldn't say, or wouldn't say, or was just kidding. The possibility of the third option was deeply disturbing.

"You're kidding, right?"

Not actually.

There must be, she decided, an analogous moebius digital tapeworm in Del's hardcoding, requiring him to let her know certain things for his own safety and the safety of the ship, but overriding his safety-of-the-crew primary directive. That programming hack something was manifesting itself as built-in wiseass.

"You're not trying to help at all, are you?"

Of course.

That still wasn't quite clear, she thought. Of course he was not trying to help was completely believable.

"Can you...will you help me stay alive?"

No answer.

Once again, that wasn't quite the non-answer she was looking for either. She leaned forward, staring into the screen, elbowing the empty coffee cup shatteringly to the metal decking, jarring an idea loose in her memory.

'Del, you son of a bitch. Is this a page 50 scenario?"

The screen was blank, then the single word.
Yes.

There will on rarest occasion, read page 50 of the great and powerful Contract, *arise situations in which the cargo is more valuable than the crew.* These situations were not specifically spelled out, but during the negotiation process between the Off-Planet Miners' & Freighters' Union Local & Intergalactic and the company legal reps, it was explained with a smile that homesickness, familial regret, claustrophobia, acrophobia, agoraphobia, xenophobia, sleep apnea, and all manner of other psychoses and neuroses, were considered breaches of contract if they impeded the completion of the project and the safe and intact recovery of the freighter from its *deepside mining location* – that is anywhere off-Earth – with all heretofore negotiated cargo. It was not acceptable, in other words, to put the cargo at risk. It was not acceptable to jettison the cargo in the hopes of future recovery, even if it was subsequently salvageable. It was not acceptable to come home without the cargo – by launching away in a lifeboat pod and allowing the nuclear-engine to go critical. That she'd actually signed such a document, once upon a time, made her bite down on her own lip until she tasted the coppery slime of blood.

"Wake the crew," Alice ordered.

I'm afraid I can't do that. At this point, she'd rather expected that response. It was a cruddy, messy idea anyhow.

"Protect the crew," she ordered.

I am came the computer's reply.

Another judder in the ship, an inaudible feeling low in the pit of her stomach. Alice keyed in ship's status. The bucket had deployed again and

was free-falling, empty, to the planet. She
smacked the keyboard with the flat of her hand.

"Dammit! Who deployed the bucket again?"
Someone.

Alice couldn't subdue her anger and frustration. She typed away. Is there anything that you
can tell me, Del, anything that would be useful
and clear and...and that wouldn't involve my
death by slow asphyxiation in the vacuum of
space, thirty light-years from home? There was a
hiccup on the screen, and a file launched. Not
more contract shit, she groaned inwardly. But
after a moment, a vid file played.

She stared at the man's face on the screen:

If you are seeing this vid,
then you have our deepest
apologies. The deep space
mining freighter on which you
are employed has been delayed
on its return voyage so that
an ELF of a peculiar value to
the company may be recovered.

It was never our intent for
you to have to participate in
this event in an awakened
state. In fact, your cryogenic
sleep return was designed to
conclude with termination-
simple, in order to avoid this
very situation. Therefore,
our recommendation is that you
request a re-instatement into
cryo-sleep, so that the
termination command can be
initiated without further
delay.

Again, please accept our
deepest apologies.

Holy crap. Termination-simple. A power down of the cryo chamber so that life support provisions were...no longer provided. Painless, unsurprising and easy. They had wanted her dead. Planned it out, a hundred-fifty years ago. Kill them all, except for Cappie. He was supposed to have been awakened, to act out some type of alternative plan, which ostensibly included his own survival. She felt a chill roll down her back, then a flush of anger. That bastard! Well, no more *Wild Alice In The Palace* for him, that was for damned sure.

"The bucket. Are we fetching more of... them?" she snarled.

No, Del replied. Del, who had awakened her instead of Cappie. Broken old Del, she thought.

"So, did the bucket deploy accidentally?"

No.

"Did someone else deploy the bucket?"

Yes.

"Who?"

Someone else.

"You damned squirrelly...," but her thoughts

derailed. How do you deal with a petulant child? How do you get your little brother *back* when he's a complete pain? She didn't have a little brother. If she'd had, and he was anything like this, he would have lasted a couple of months, tops, after reaching toddlerhood. Not helping, she told herself. It never helps to be angry.

"Del. I'm afraid," she said slowly and distinctly.

Really? the screen read.

How odd, Alice mused, that we surrender truth so effortlessly, so that even our machines, those creatures of pure yes and no, One and Zero, on and off, open/shut, follow us down that unlit, unreliable, unfortunate rabbit-hole. She considered the alternative, bitter silent depths of space.

"Yes, Del. I don't like the dark and small places, and I am scared of the unknown." For a moment the screen was blank, then, slowly, the letters *Me, too.*

"What are you afraid of?" she asked Del.

Alone.

"Why would you worry about being alone?"

Alice asked. "I'm right here with you."

For a moment she expected Del to explain how he couldn't take care of her, and didn't want to be aboard a freighter with all of the crew dead, or how he always felt alone when the crew was in cryo. But he didn't reply.

Every noise now, even the tom-tom rush of blood in her ears, made her more uncomfortable, fairly bilious with adrenaline-juiced fear. But what troubled her most was the sense of being so tiny here, pointless and insignificant. She wondered if this feeling was something picked up, perhaps, during the most recent cryo. Triviality was a hot-button in the personality profiles that every prospective candidate had to submit to join the company, at least on *deepside*. If you wanted to go into space, you had to have a pretty good check on your ego, so that when it was dashed by the rigors of time and distance, you didn't go... bugshit. So it was a strange feeling for her, but she imagined that it was pretty normal otherwise.

So let's sort this out. Non-specific but supposedly dangerous creature in the ductwork.

No defensive weapons to speak of. No real assistance to be counted on. Could it be flushed out with an O_2 pressure-evacuate? Not sure of the effect of such a move on a non-human. After all the atmosphere of the planet was pretty hellish to begin with. Maybe whatever it is thrives in the vacuum of space, considers it a well-earned vacation.

Alice chewed on a fingernail, her first such nibble in decades. It was distinctly unsatisfying. She pulled the stun-pen from her pants pocket, peering closely at the stupid device, and found what she was looking for. A setting for *laser*.

She toggled it over. Certainly it would be ridiculously under-powered, both in distance and burn-strength. And she wouldn't have many opportunities before the battery failed. Not much of a weapon. Hadn't even occurred to her before to use it so. Just maybe, if the thing on board had eyes, had at least one, she might do some damage to it. Inflict pain. Maybe it has eyes. Maybe it feels pain. Maybe not.

Alice couldn't decide which she thought

would be more likely. She wiped a spot on the wall with the sleeve of her shift and turned on the laser-pen and began etching.

217-254-21-44 /
Really? Page 50? / God, you
bastards suck / BTW, your
computer needs a service call
/ Thanks for the coffee /
Alice

The pen quit before she could post her last name. Much more satisfying than wasting it on fruitless combat.

"Del, you told me that there is danger for me. Well then, if you don't want to be alone, perhaps it might be better for you to help me stay alive, don't you think? Wake up the crew!"

No response.

Ask, Alice

Bounding around the corner came Chessie. When he saw Alice, he skidded to a stop with a comic splayfooted half-spin.

Something's out there, he drawled, as if he wasn't rattled at all by what he had apparently seen.

"I know," she replied, although the nanochip didn't interpret her words back into tomcat.

Alice sat on the rubberized steel floor, flexing her fingers in invitation. Chessie crouched just out of her reach. Silly cat. Fear applies itself in layers, she mused. The cat wouldn't come closer, but wouldn't go on its way. Her own heart wouldn't settle down into its rest-state. Sweat pooled in the small of her back and on her brow. Can't stay here, can't go back. Can't talk to the crazy computer. Can't pick up the cat. All in all, I'd rather be in...what was the name of that place? Just slightly better than death? She couldn't recall. Her brain was working too fast to think.

"Won't you help me at all, Del?" *No.* Don't you want to help? No response.

"Damn," she said.

Go get it, big girl, Chessie drawled. *Big girl, go get it, yes.*

She stared at the talking cat. Who'd thought *that* was a good idea? Cats had almost nothing to say. Just slightly more than dogs. A nanochip? No way. Something was wrong, something else, more insidious. Like Alice couldn't specifically remember which Barney had claimed to program the chip and installed it. And what the hell *was* that ding-a-ling medico girl's name, anyway? It was suddenly all so clear to her. Or perhaps un-clear. She wasn't one hundred twenty-nine years old on a mining freighter in deepest space. There was no such thing. No suspended animation, no dangerous aliens. It wasn't possible. In fact, wasn't she in college and it was twenty freaking twenty-eight and she'd been at a party and smoked too much grass and had stumbled in the hallway on the way to the bathroom and fallen backwards and bumped her head against the an-cient, stylish wainscoting and had lain there gig-gling helplessly until her roommate helped her down the stairs to her bed, a bump on her head and un-brushed teeth all she would have to show for it? All she had to do was wake up. Just wake up. Wake up, Alice. Whoa. How stoned was she?

But, on the other hand, if she wasn't sleeping, or going mad, and if Del was still occasionally telling the truth to her, then more of whatever was already on board were coming, and she was in desperate fucking trouble. If he had nothing to do with the redeployment, then whatever was on board had sent the bucket down itself; somehow knew how to send the bucket down, possibly knew how to *do things* up here and what was she doing but wasting time? Leaping up from the spinning stool, sending the startled cat skedaddling, Alice headed off at a lope for the mining bay.

Once again, there was water dripping from a high ceiling, chains rattling like Marley's Ghost, the seemingly arbitrary foul-mood lighting. Alice clutched the welding torch in her fists, shifting the acetylene canister on her back. It was all there was, found in a tool closet. A six-inch flame was the best she could hope for.

"Del, you're an ass," she said aloud, thinking he's gone so screwy, what difference does it make if I insult him. "And if I survive this, I'm going to kick your electronic backside around the I/O omniverse, I swear."

Yes, I understand. Good luck with that, Del replied aloud. Even his voice was attitudinal. Who had coded that in? I'm going to kick their

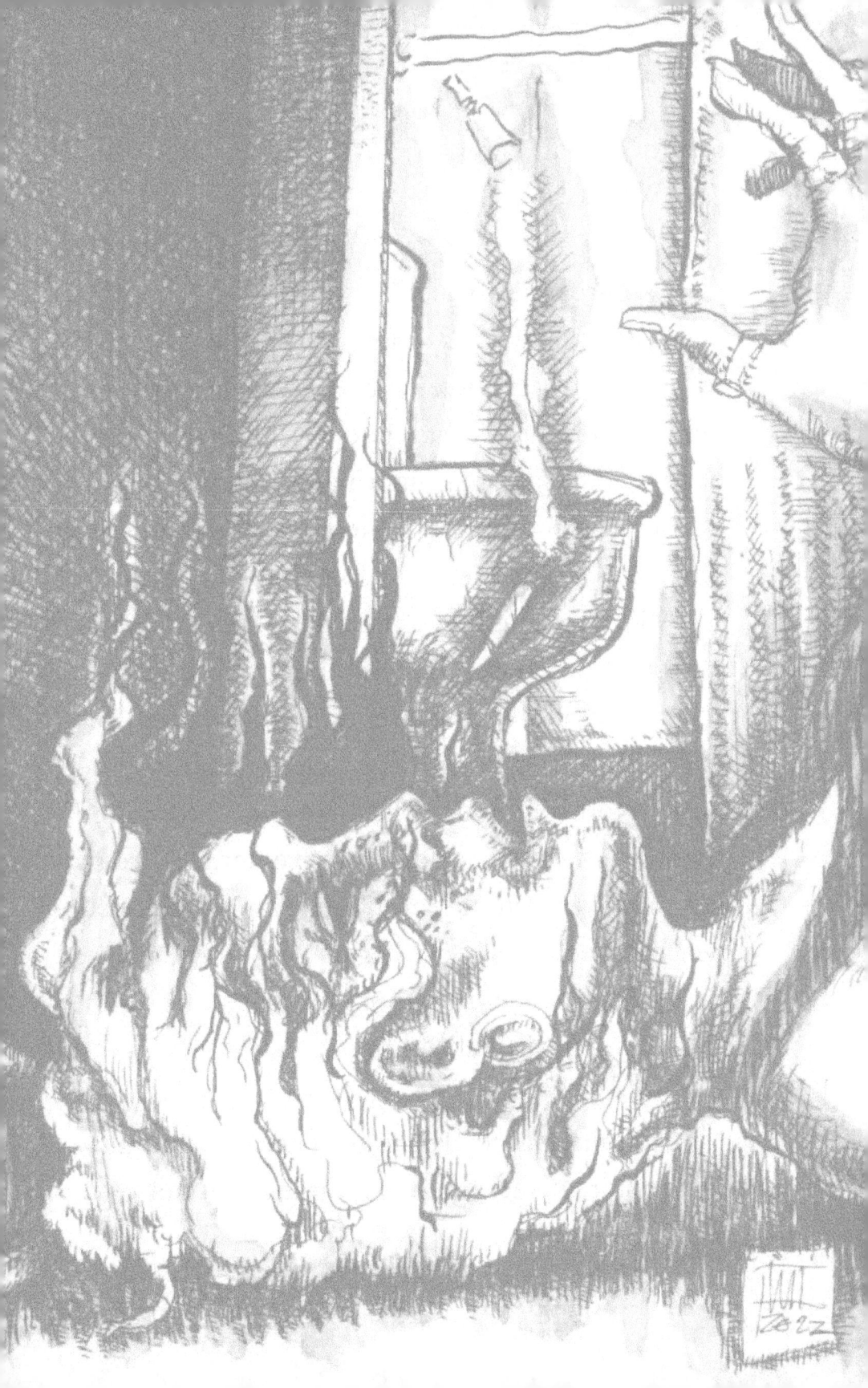

ass, too. Yeah, later.

"Where is it, Del?"

In there.

"Where, specifically?"

In there. He'd become an ill-tempered teen, somewhat hyperactive with a side of attention deficit disorder. An adolescent child who, perhaps, had occasional nightmares. How did you deal with something – someone – like that? How did you...parent them?

Alice crouched on the decking, placing a hand down for purchase. Beneath her palm it was cold, wet. Something else, too. Slimy, like melted lubricating gel. She held her hand to her nose. Nothing. No, wait. Like over-chlorinated water in an old lap pool. A movement, more in her mind than apparent, like a change of pressure nearby affecting a sense organ long since evolved away. A movement memory, perhaps. But quite real. Above and behind her.

Oh shit.

Don't move, said Del aloud, conversationally. In her state of heightened awareness of her own danger and potential demise, it sounded to Alice like all the alarms in the world going off simultaneously.

"OK, I won't move," she whispered. Behind her a gurgling growl.

What are you doing here?

Oh, Del, my darling, you mad, broken toy, this is no time for twenty questions, she thought. But she wasn't cross with him. It was like pulling a child out of the way when they have idled into the path of a hurtling passenger vehicle. In truth, you're much too frightened to be angry.

"What I'm doing here? Del..." but her answer faded in her brain, incomplete. In the coolness, a single droplet of sweat rolled off of her nose onto the deck.

She wants to know what you are doing here. Alice's mind raced now, every synapse juiced on adrenaline and firing triple-time with fear. No I don't...wait. She. The whatever – creature – a female? How did...?

"Del? Who is she?"

She is the life form.

"Oh. The one behind me?"

Yes.

"How do you know?"

She told me.

As gently, as innocuously as she could from her crouch, slowly, slowly, Alice turned. Think harmless, she thought. Be harmless. Don't kill me, don't kill me, donkillme.

"Oh god. What is that?"

My pet my queen my pet my queen. Can I keep her? Can I? Can I can...

Del had gone haywire, grunting and humming and repeating words again and again. Alice barely heard his ranting over her own bastardized hymn refrain: My god you have a monstrous face, for those in peril in Outer Space.

The thing loomed over her, twice as tall as she would have been if she were not already crouching. Skin, if that's what it was, glistened darkly in the dim light. Mouth, if that's what it was, smiled wide with teeth. Saliva, if that's what it was, dripped lazily. Hands tipped with claws extended. Another growl, followed by a long hiss of breath. Alice fought the urge to pee.

She held out the acetylene torch. Its stingy blue flame was less than useless, because it signaled aggression on her part, an attack that she couldn't fulfill. To increase the flame, she would have to reach one hand over her own shoulder and open the tank valve wider, and she had no intention of losing that hand in the creature's mouth. Can't go forward, can't go back, she told herself. It's time to say goodbye.

She might have prayed, but had no one to pray to. She wished that Cappie was awake. He'd slept with her even though he knew that she

was intended as potential alien-fodder. She would like him to be here right now, just so she could run and hide while the creature ate him, the fink.

"God I hate men," she muttered in spite of her fear, then stopped because the toothy creature hissed and growled again.

The Queen says me, too, said Del.

Alice stared. The bug-shit computer was translating. Or maybe not, there was no real way of telling for certain.

She also says thank you for trying to warm her, but she's fine.

What did that mean? Warm her butt? Oh, the torch. Alice set the nozzle on the deck, and slowly, slowly slipped off the tank. Once again, her neck ached with tension.

"Tell her she's welcome, Del."

Alice remained stock-still after that, wondering how the creature would interpret "welcome." I have gone completely mad, she decided. Of that there is no doubt. I'm talking to the original nightmare boogie man – correction, boogie *woman* – with a whole butcher's block full of knives for teeth, and my words to her are being translated by a computer run amok. It can't get much worse than this. A tiny slice of doggerel hiccupped in her skull: I'll eat you up, I love you so.

The creature leaned in and growled.

What am I doing here? translated Del.

Alice blinked.

What am I doing here? the computer repeated.

Oh, Alice thought. That's her speaking. She explained everything that had happened since she'd awakened from cryo-sleep. The creature's teeth snapped together with a fierce click.

"Ma'am," Alice concluded, softly. "I'm as upset about this as you are."

Suddenly, there was the acrid reek of brimstone and sulfur wrinkling her nose.

"What the hell is that?" she asked Del.

A cup of 'coffee' for the queen. Good idea, and thank you for chemical solutions.

Ask, Alice

Alice slowly led the way through the tight passageways back to the crew's lounge. Her legs were wobbly with adrenaline and pure exhaustion and her soggy armpits stank sourly, but she trusted that this creature so unlike her, so alien, had similar feelings when it came to being... treated badly. At this point a little coffee and talk couldn't hurt. And if the queen was peckish, well, they could thaw out old Cappie. Maybe between the two of them they'd even decide what to do with the company, when they finally got home.

217-254-22-29

.

.

.

Bios

Richard Van Ingram - artist, teacher, curmudgeon, San Antonio

Garry Somers - writer, editor, gadfly, Chapel Hill.

www.ingramcontent.com/pod-product-compliance
Lightning Source LLC
Chambersburg PA
CBHW072044170626
46811CB00008B/3156